THE UNCERTAIN LAND

The Works of Patrick O'Brian

The Aubrey/Maturin Novels
In order of publication

MASTER AND COMMANDER
POST CAPTAIN
HMS SURPRISE
THE MAURITIUS COMMAND
DESOLATION ISLAND
THE FORTUNE OF WAR
THE SURGEON'S MATE
THE IONIAN MISSION
TREASON'S HARBOUR
THE FAR SIDE OF THE WORLD
THE REVERSE OF THE MEDAL
THE LETTER OF MARQUE
THE THIRTEEN-GUN SALUTE
THE NUTMEG OF CONSOLATION
CLARISSA OAKES
THE WINE-DARK SEA
THE COMMODORE
THE YELLOW ADMIRAL
THE HUNDRED DAYS
BLUE AT THE MIZZEN
THE FINAL UNFINISHED VOYAGE OF JACK AUBREY

Novels

TESTIMONIES
THE CATALANS
THE GOLDEN OCEAN
THE UNKNOWN SHORE
RICHARD TEMPLE
CAESAR
HUSSEIN
THE ROAD TO SAMARCAND

Tales

THE LAST POOL
THE WALKER
LYING IN THE SUN
THE CHIAN WINE
COLLECTED SHORT STORIES
BEASTS ROYAL

Biography

PICASSO
JOSEPH BANKS

Anthology

A BOOK OF VOYAGES

PATRICK O'BRIAN

The Uncertain Land

and Other Poems

HarperCollins*Publishers*

HarperCollins*Publishers* Ltd
1 London Bridge Street,
London SE1 9GF
www.harpercollins.co.uk

First published by HarperCollins*Publishers* 2019
1

A catalogue record for this book is available from the British Library

ISBN: 978-0-00-826134-4

Set in Sabon by Palimpsest Book Production Limited, Falkirk,
Stirlingshire

Printed and bound in the UK by
CPI Group (UK) Ltd, Croydon CR0 4YY

MIX
Paper from
responsible sources
FSC www.fsc.org **FSC™ C007454**

This book is produced from independently certified FSC™ paper to
ensure responsible forest management.

For more information visit: www.harpercollins.co.uk/green

Contents

Foreword by Nikolai Tolstoy   ix

Part I: Poems

Blitz poetry   1
'The sea and the sky are silent'   5
Mrs Koren   6
'The harsh dry polished rattle'   7
'You will come to it'   8
The Olive Harvest   9
The Inine   11
tibi donum offero   12
A present   13
French verses   14
   Mal du pays   14
   Le bois des oiseaux   14
   Espagnols exilés   15
'A dog bit his master'   16
Goat   17
Looking towards the south   18
Foxes surprised   19
Epitaph   20
February   21
The Deep Gold of a Pomegranate-Tree   22
The Cypress Tree   23
Meads no more   24
The Lagoon   25
A Lycéen   27
In Upper Leeson Street   28
How to lay a mine   30
The far side of the pass   32

August, Sun-impaled   33
Words from the bottom of a river   34
Croagh Patrick   36
A T'ang Landscape Remembered   37
Song   38
Farewell, my sin I have enjoyed you   39
A man under his impulsion   40
David danced before the ark   41
The falling of the leaves   43
Dear Mona Fitzpatrick '32 (or '3)   44
The theft   45
The electric light failing   46
Youth gone   47
Giving up smoking   48
Diego   49
Spaniards Exiled   52
The Captain and the Stock   53
To the hermitage and down, refreshed   55
Waiting for money in a far country   58
In Madame Ponsalié's garden   60
Walk by the sea to see wonders   62
The raven   64
The young listless man   65
From the Welsh   66
Snowdon for the sunrise   67
The wine-dark sea   69
The bad day   70
Sterne   71
The Pleiades on Christmas Eve   72
The apology   73
Dead hours of louring justification, a desert of time   75
Myself a young man read a poem   76
The uncertain land   78
Silver-haired charm and urbanity   81
Winter in Foreign Parts   82

Obsèques   83
The dark figures   85
'Is true the rat'   86
The duty of pleasure   87
Poulp: or, the Medusa a Toy   88
Grey and white   89
No smoking: the second day   90
Pray, Luv, forgive me my sourness   91
The Mandrake   92
For Louise's visitors' book   94
'Clouds over clouds'   95
'Walking on the high mountain'   97
'Help my understanding, Lady'   98
'Down through the vines'   99
Collioure   100
'Long, straight, the steel lines'   101
'If I could go back into my dream'   102
'Loose-bellied, grey'   103
Old Men   104
'When your lance fails'   105

Part II: Drafts

The Sardana for the First Time   109
'Yesterday an old husband'   111
'Whereas in Jewry came a star'   112
'Not that a hard-roed herring should presume'   113
'The pattering of rain'   114
'The cry of buzzards in the sky'   115
'Vicious intromission'   116
Forbear O Venus pray forbear   117
A halt on the Trans-Siberian   118
'When my Muse and Chian Veins vie'   119
The sorrow & woe   120
Boars   121

Night walking   129
'On the mountain I have quite a good sense   131
    of direction'
The True-born Englishman   132
'Sun sloping through the cypresses'   135
Labuntur anni (The advancing years)   136
'Peace; a great lawn that small, fat feet'   137
The hard winter   138
'An old thin tall man'   139
What the hell do you know about poverty?   140
'The north wind low over the house'   141
'High on the cold mountain road'   142
'I went out in a night of tearing wind'   143
'A wheeling buzzard lifting to the sun'   145
'Thoughts that range from anger and revenge'   146
'Of France and of the knowledge of that land'   147
Captivity   149
'When a dry heart sets a bleeding'   151
Loud-mouthed neighbours through the floor   153
'For Jojo's livre d'or 85'   154

Acknowledgements   155
Index of first lines   157

Foreword

I do not know when Patrick first began composing poetry. However, I strongly suspect that it was during his frequently lonely adolescence, when he was cooped up largely alone in his father's successive homes. He was from an early age a voracious reader. He was also a passionate devotee of the natural world, and during the three years he lived as an adolescent boy at Lewes in Sussex he spent long happy hours wandering along the banks of the nearby river Ouse, and along the sands of the beach below the towering white cliffs at Seaford. Much of his poetry is concerned with limpid depictions of animals, especially birds, and delicate descriptions of the landscape with which he was familiar.

The earliest specimens of his poetry to have survived are, in contrast, robustly humorous (even mildly erotic) – which will come as no surprise to readers of the Aubrey-Maturin epic. During the Blitz in 1940–41 he and my mother drove ambulances in Chelsea, which was heavily bombed by Luftwaffe aeroplanes offloading their remaining bombs before returning homeward above the moonlit Thames. Patrick entertained his fellow workers in the ambulance station at 18 Danvers Street by acting as unofficial bard of the unit. There he composed a lively anthem for the denizens of number 22 Station of the London Auxiliary Ambulance Service. He also concocted a poetic narrative recounting the nocturnal adventures of my mother's faithful dachshund, Miss Patz, who sneaks out of her lodgings to join the regulars at the Black Lion pub around the corner from the ambulance station, and moves on to one of the many shady little drinking clubs which characterised the perilous Chelsea of those days. I suspect that Miss Patz's exploits reflected in some degree those of her adventurous owner. My mother, in addition, assisted with the fluent German and French sections of the poem, being fluent in both languages.

For four years after the War my parents lived in a tiny cottage in the mountains of Snowdonia, where their fare depended in large part on Patrick's skill with rod and gun. They were also avid followers of the local foxhounds, a hunt conducted on foot amid wildly dramatic mountain scenery. There, as Patrick's novel *Three Bear Witness** attests, he paid minute attention to landscape and wildlife. I find it hard to believe that he did not also commemorate them in poetry at the same time, although all of his muse that survives is his cheerful ode to a generous American lady who sent them tins of marmalade in 1946.

In 1949 he and my mother migrated to Collioure in the south of France. During the more rewarding decades which ensued, Patrick regularly jotted down poems in little notebooks and on odd sheets of paper. Among the earliest verse surviving from that period are allusions to the wild and rugged land-scape they had left behind them, which was not dissimilar to that of the Pyrenees towering above the little town.

Many of Patrick's salient characteristics are revealed in this collection: his recurring fear of death, love of local scenery, and careful perception of the patient labours of the local inhabitants. Although he was broadly apolitical, in his poem *Espagnols exilés* he manifests poignant sympathy for Spanish Republicans who had fled across the frontier in 1939, a residue of whom lingered on in Collioure after my parents' arrival.

---

* Later reissued under the title *Testimonies*.

However, it should not be thought that his themes are all melancholy. He cherished a copy of Edward Lear's poems, given to me by a fond great-aunt for my fourth birthday, which my mother abstracted shortly afterwards when she departed our family home to live with Patrick. 'A dog bit his master', composed not long after their arrival at Collioure, provides a fine specimen of Patrick's love of the absurd.

In the following year he composed his poem 'In Upper Leeson Street', which nostalgically evokes his memorable stay in Dublin in 1937, where he completed his precocious novel *Hussein*. Although even in private he talked little about his former life (save, I assume, to my mother), it is clear that in his mind he dwelt much on their early days of adventurous privation, as well as images of people and places lovingly stored in his memory. The earliest allusions are to be found in the reverie 'If I could go back into my dream', which if I am not mistaken draws upon childish fancies of wild beasts frequenting the streets, areas, and corners of the London with which he was familiar when living there as a small boy of five.

Although Patrick devoted much care to poetic composition, much of it does not appear even to have been submitted for publication. Unlike his prose, which he generally looked upon with justified approval, he quite frequently expressed hesitant reservations about the value of his poetry. As he noted in his diary in October 1978, 'More work on poems, but doubt keeps creeping in & as I wrote on one of them, simplicity can come v close to silliness'. But he was rigorously self-critical, and I for one find his poetry delightful.

He was strongly drawn to the genre, and possessed a particular penchant for the writings of Chaucer, which he possessed in Tyrwhitt's handsome two-volume edition (1798). Time and again, when relaxing with a drink after the day's labours were done, he would return to the ebullient Father of English Poetry with zestful pleasure. When I stayed with my parents in the days of my youth, we would follow supper by taking it in turns to read aloud our favourite poems accompanied by the shrilling of cicadas in the darkened vineyard. For some reason, this congenial practice was later abandoned, but it was doubtless continued when Patrick was alone with my mother.*

In September 1978 Patrick noted in his diary:

> My poems discourage me: too personal, often too trifling. There are some I like that would do for general consumption but probably not enough to make a book.

However, he had earlier noted:

> These last 2 days I've been looking through my poems, with the idea of picking out enough of those that do not make me blush for a volume: many I had quite forgotten & some surprised me agreeably.

Although he sent a batch shortly afterwards to his sympathetic literary agent Richard Scott Simon, only a handful saw the light of publication during Patrick's lifetime. Now, however, this handsome collection has been brought together, containing both polished versions and drafts that for one reason or another were left in an unfinished state, which I do not doubt will give Patrick's legion of admirers around the world the pleasure they afford me.

NIKOLAI TOLSTOY, 2018

---

* This was not always easy during their early years living in the bustling town of Collioure. As my mother noted in her diary: 'Patrick tried to read a T.S.E[liot]. poem [*Burnt Norton*] aloud yesterday but was drowned by the noise in the rue. Both boiled this morning as cats howling kept us from sleeping'.

Part I: Poems

Blitz poetry

Lines of unpredictable merit written on the back of Miss Patz, a rough-haired Dachshundin in the year of Grace a thousand nine hundred and forty-one, on Wednesday, the eighth day of January, at about half after one in the afternoon, it being a cold day, dismal with half molten snow.

The people of this [Chelsea ambulance] station are
    disconsolate and rude,
All English to the tonsils, and filled with British
    phlegm.
They blow their noses horribly, and between the blast is
    spewed
A flux of ghastly small-talk. Why, O God, did you
    make them?
★¿Was other clay not handy?
Was there nothing else to please?
O Lord that gave us brandy
And lamb and fresh green peas
★¿Why did You turn your hand to these?

The last line is (I think) an Alexandrine,
which is very clever indeed, probably.

★That is affected, I must admit. ¿But am
I inferior to a Spaniard? ¡No!

In dispraise of the Personnel of 22 St[ation].
    L.A.A.S.*

---

* London Auxiliary Ambulance Service.

The people of this station are disconsolate and rude
they are English to the tonsils, and with British phlegm
     embued
In proof of this opinion to their handkerchiefs I point
And not only to their kerchiefs, but oyster eyes and
     rheumy joint.
But also to their tempers, habitually vile
The fruit of grave distempers and coagulated bile.
All wart-hogs in comparison are quite high-souled and mild
Which leads to the conclusion that the better beasts are
     wild.

This may be sung (though the notion is grim)
To the tune of a well-known American hymn.
viz., or vide licet, if you should prefer the word
Mine eyes have seen the glory of the coming of the
     Lord. . .

[Miss Patz]
Patz went out in the dead of the night,
in the dead of the night went she.
But first she carefully put out the light,
And closed the door with a key.

[Miss Patz's invitation to the pub]
Sie sagte sich «Im ein Augenblick»
Ich werde haben ein grosse Trink.
Und so in kleiner
Moment werdet in meiner
Turn, zwei-drei steiner

2

Sein, oder bier als wein.
Gut. Geh'ich nach Klub.
Nein; erst hab ich lust für ein Pub.
She went quite straight to the Lion called Black*
Tossed down a quick pint, and never looked back
For a wicked old Owl, who took his dram raw
Determined to try the truth of the saw . . .
mark the Saw.

   In wommin vinident ['full of wine'] is no defence,
     ðus knoweth lechours by experience.

                              Dan C[haucer].

So he plied her with whiskey, with gin and with rum
And said that he wished she would instantly come
To a very fine party to be held at a club
So complaisant and willing she then left the pub.
At the club she encountered a motley crew
Hard-drinking and raffish and lecherous too
They drank bottles of whiskey and magnums of gin
Till Patz felt uncertain what state she was in.
The Owl broke off in the midst of a tale
(It was singularly dirty – exclusively male)
And said 'Liebe Fraülein, what makes you so pale?
Come, drink up a glass of red pepper and ale.'
She said 'it's my head, the air, heat and the smoke,'
And giggled like one who has just made a joke.
The Owl thought, 'Aha, now may I eat grass,
But this is the time when I make the first pass.'
And through his foul mind there passed devious shapes
Of libidinous bitches and lecherous apes.

---

* The Black Lion pub in Church Street, Chelsea.

[Jetzt kommt er bei Patz,*
Und flüßtert ganz leise
'Heraus liegt ein Auto,
Kommst Du für ein Reise?'
'Ach nein! Du alt Teufel!
Wie kannst du mir's fragen?
Ich weiß schon gehörts
L.C.C. dieser Wagon!'
Alors les autres
Se mettaient à rire
En se moquant de l'hibou
Qui ne savait quoi dire.
Il saisit d'un coup
Une bouteille de vin,
La vidait toute suite
Et la jettait du main.
'Je paris', dit-il,
'Je ne quitterai pas
Avant que la chienne
Se sert dans mes bras'.]

---

* The concluding responses in German and French are pencilled in Mary
O'Brian's hand.

4

'The sea and the sky are silent'

The sea and the sky are silent:
they wait.
The sea and the sky are silent:
the girl is late.

The sea and the sky are silent:
the girl is late.
The sea and the sky are waiting:
let her come to her fate.

Mrs Koren

Couplets in favour of Mrs W. Koren, who sent (per JBC)* jam to the
O'Brians [at Collioure] in time of dearth

All Attic virtues, beauty, wisdom, wit,
Take which you will, she doth excel in it
All these and yet one more th'Atlantic dame
Hath to illumine her noble spouse's name,
Mark there the Greek with Chian wine and oil
Comes bearing gifts, and see how vain his toil.
Yet here Transpontine Ceres freely sends
Imprison'd comfits, Polemarchus' blends, . . .
And dreams not fear nor anger (see above)
But grateful intercessions and our love

The pallid bread glows purple, and the dew
Of anxious gleed bespreads each wizen'd brow
Encrimson'd mouths gape sated at the last
Such admirable tins of jam as these
Are apt to promote international pese
May Heaven reward Mrs Koren
Who is undoubtedly a pearl among women.
The recipient of jam were [sic] undoubtedly a moron

---

* Jack Christopher

6

'The harsh dry polished rattle'

The harsh dry polished rattle of the palm fronds
stirring in the breeze. I had supposed
But not our London sparrow, magpie, crow
Still less the stars by night, our Plough, old Bear
the same Orion, Rigal, Altair there
and through the trees the shining Procyon.

'You *will* come to it'

You will come to it
Do not suppose their motions pantomime
because the thing they dig is dark, unseen
the mattock and the shovel swing in time
a near approach will show you what they mean.

The Olive Harvest

Cold from the silent leaden sky, unmoving, full of
  snow.
Cold, and the sounds far on the smoky air –
the rackle, hoe in stones, the stoney vineyard high
and the working man much farther than the sound
All through the terraced valley, sounds.
The vines are bare, the spare leaves redden:
they prune: and everywhere they grub with shining
  tools
And in the silence sounds – on silence beads, the
  sounds.

Now there are women.
gabbling
Where are the women? There
gabbling
above the road, the vines, the olives
the prim the graceful olive trees
the women picking there the olives
a tilted plane, the trees, the women
and then the sky, one-coloured, leaden.
Neat, clear, unworldly, Pieter Brueghel.

I do not like to see the women.
Black. Not shining. Black entirely.
head to foot, and cheesey faces.
Eager, hard and clacking voices: and the hands
are deadly white for ever groping,
They stand as high, and monstrously
they stand as high, as does the tree.

Their hands
are deadly white, for ever groping.
Emasculating
in the trees.

The Inine

The winter hillside
brown
sharp, clear, distinct
and figures running
tiny, shortened, struggling with space.
A plouff of smoke
is drifting on the field
larger: larger, vague: and now the bang
the echoes clapping in the hills, hard hills,
and now the rain
reversed: the rattle
cruel ripping tearing hail
of stones that fell
in time disturbed, before.

tibi donum offero

I am poor about loving, so
tibi donum offero
It is a present as you see
extractum ex operi
quod ex libro domini
extractum est, alas by me
theft it was, but theft or no
tibi donum offero.

A present

A present is chiefly a fragment, a token
of affection and love.
And then there is the strong pleasure of giving
a visible proof of unbroken
kindness and more
But, the interchanging pleasure apart
and discounted
A ring is a token of marriage; a book
of the spirit that made it.
and a present of love.
But the marriage is more than the ring
and the mind than the book.

French verses

Mal du pays

Les vignes, les chênes-lièges, oliviers et thym
les Catalans
le sein
vierge du Canigou
le vent vif des montagnes
et tous
ces pics fiers, hautains
d'Espagne.

J'avais prévu.
Mais pas le moineau anglais, ni la pie
le corbeau parlant gallois, même ici.
Et renard, je t'ai déjà vu
t'ai chassé, là, dans mon pays.

Et à travers les feuilles semées
(étranges feuilles des palmiers)
vieilles étoilles, là notr' Charrue
Rigel, Altair: à perte de vue
nos douces Pléïades, les mêmes que celles
qui hantent les gens de Camberwell.

Le bois des oiseaux

vent qui chant dans le bois des oiseaux
et vert le soleil dans les feuilles, jeunes feuilles.
Courbé, courbé sur les pierres
les pierres vertes de Coed Tŷ

yeux fixes, aveugles sur la terre
la terre moussue de Coed Tŷ
je tenais dans mes mains la peine
la peine, la peine, cher Dieu la peine
la peine atroce là, dans mon coeur.

Espagnols exilés[*]

Une femme qui chante
et dans la rue étroite soleil qui fait
des ombres durs, rigides et rectilignes
rien ne bouge
mais dans la rue
le Chant qui tombe, se meurt, gitane
à fendre le coeur, mi corazón.
Oh querido, mi corazón.

Ils chantent ici, les Espagnols
dans le pays d'autres, pays étranger,
dans un autre pays qui n'est pas le leur.

---

[*] Republican refugees in Collioure. See p. 52 for the translation

'A dog bit his master'

A dog bit his master
who in order to leave to posterity an account of this
   disaster
took an unusually large piece of pink-and-yellow
   mottled alabaster
which, having been found at the mouth of a Pyrenean
   river
did not, by that unforeseen circumstance, cost him
   anything at all: not so much as a stiver.

Goat

A man long used to affection (a roof, as it were;
a condition of being)
Withers strangely when it is removed.
His days grow incommensurably long
He abbreviates his nights with pills Guaranteed
    Nepenthe four new pence
Shrivels, old and surly, says Do not say
I stabbed myself with my own lance.
Do not say 'You in the person of an aging goat
put the fire to your own thatch'
I do not feel the want of shelter any less

Looking towards the south

Beyond my window the mountain hangs like a curtain
pinned at one end by the castle.
Vineyards almost half way up it, vines in rows;
then a dull-green and tawny waste.
Partridges breed in the wasteland and call throughout
   the spring
asparagus grows there wild
and as the year wears on
a snake-eagle rides steady on the wind
gazing down with orange eyes:
august moons rise behind the castle
and in the winter the dog-star
heaves up, a splendid lamp.

Foxes surprised

We looked over the cliff and there were foxes
little foxes playing among the boulders
skipping wrangling scratching their fleas
and the vixen laying her length in the sun.
In and out among the boulders, tag, king of the castle
like so many lambs
and one threw a crab in the air.
A sound, perhaps a whiff of scent on the eddy
and instantly they were hard old foxes
hard wary old foxes without a second's transition.
They vanished into the rocks and the cove
was utterly silent: rocks, the heat dancing
and a calm sea stretching away and away.

Epitaph

I too walked in churchyards and spelt out the stones
the directory of a world that I should never know
I too was quite immortal then
And never even heard their universal cry
'Profit by what little sun is left
Eat up all your bread and wine.'

February

The snow has almost vanished from Las Nao Fons
The forest is no longer grey with cold
Down here the robin sings at breakfast-time
a red bosom in a could of almond-flowers:
the dim glow of violets beyond the orange-tree
and an early partridge calling on the hill.

The Deep Gold of a Pomegranate-Tree

The deep gold of a pomegranate-tree
glowing in the clipped frame of cypresses
on an almond-branch
a robin whistling quietly to itself
light flooding down from the high autumnal sky
and from the vineyards gold flooding up to the grey
    autumnal sky.
In the Massane wood blue mushrooms are pushing
    through the fallen leaves.

The Cypress Tree

Long ago I planted cypress seeds
and being no gardener I plucked up the seedlings
all but one
taking them for weeds.
That one, in its neglected corner,
now stands a green flame rising twenty feet and more
capital omen capital omen.
But this summer a shabby yellowish bird
Sunken black eyes, a large pale vulgar bill
made her nest up there near the top.
She laid too late in the year and the heat of July
addled the clutch
She sits on and on in the August sun
her beak open, gasping for air.

Meads no more

The flowering meads are very well: poets used often to
　　commend
these enamelled flowering meads
and to be sure I walked on mine with considerable pleasure:
such as they were.
But it appears that a lasting quality is no part of the deal
for presently you find
that with the sly gliding malevolence of dreams these meads
have turned into a thin sheet of ice
black ice thinner
in some places than in others and everywhere unsafe
with here and there a pool on to the void.
At intervals of staring you blunder on
the sheet growing thinner thinner, mere webs of cold
and yourself dwindling in size beauty virtue sense
always on and on: no choice.

The Lagoon

We have a shifting population of flamingoes
sometimes thousands stalking together, rank upon rank so
   pink
or flying black and crimson in an undulating cloud
or gabbling like deep-voiced geese in the warm evening lake
sometimes a few score no more, deplorable umbrellas
shin-deep in cold water, leaning against the Christmas wind
their legs mauve in mud-coloured waves.
It is a country of its own, this marsh and the lagoon
although windscreens flash along a road that
divides it from the sea you sit there out of time
in an untouched primaeval bog.
Flamingoes and great rafts of coots, gulls of course, terns
and countless duck in the winter, even swans,
herons grey and purple, egrets, cormorants
these make up the mass
and this year an osprey has been there all summer
a shabby brown osprey on a given stump
doing nothing for hours but scratch and stare.
But in the spring and autumn tides the marsh
is even more full of life.
One day it will be harriers, hundreds of harriers sailing north
with black kites among them
another, ruffs and reeves among the greenshanks
and minute waders for the far far north
Grey plover, also due in the arctic tundra
Stilts.
Yet of all these none moves your heart like the peregrine
No doubt one should prefer the ringed plover or rather
   the dove

but a falcon clipping easy through the clear sky of autumn
travelling so fast, tracing a line as straight as a cord
stretched from the north horizon to the south
is in her way a trumpet-blast.
Always slightly fascist, stirred by trumpets stirred by drums
Old Adam loves a bird of prey.
Besides, that falcon in her pilgrimage
is running down to the northern edge of the summer
even to a new spring if she chooses,
and a slow earthbound creature, aging where he stands
cannot but gaze longing after that dark-eyed bird that arrow
her fierce effortless wings
flying flying
to renew her seasons to renew perhaps her youth.

A Lycéen

There was a lane behind the gasworks, they said
the sentier du gaz
where eager willing girls came in the night or
even in the twilight or by day.
shamefaced and furtive he hurried through the streets
conspicuously bowed, blushing at an encountered glance
and fetching wide detours
O how his heart beat in the sentier du gaz!
its dim warm length smelling of brimstone
And never an evening all that long summer
even when it rained
but he threaded its length five times and more
gliding into it form the main street with a despairing gasp.

In Upper Leeson Street

Three men sitting in a room on the second floor
the small square gas-fire bubbling and they drinking porter
and the smell of the bedroom and the men and their porter.
The thick air quiet between the smoke there in layers
Power on this side, Mooney there, and Keating in the
   middle
the elderly host in the basket-chair.
There were anecdotes and stories – no singing, only stories
all were obscene and fourteen were blasphemous.
In the pause while the gas-fire bubbled and the chair
   alone creaked
they searched their personal jakes and almost invented
and from the chipped whitey jug they poured the thick
   porter, the
impotent groping lascivious bastards.
Keating cocked his ear to the door, on his face a mean
   and yellow suspicion
secretly up from his chair creaking after him
flung open the door with a gregory gesture
and stared at the bloody great fiend on the far side of
   the landing
'It's a bloody great fiend' he said closing it quickly
and the rotten yellow blotched faces gaped over their porter
dirty blue teeth in their mouths the informers, three-masons.
After a while the door swelled inwards, shuddered open
   and they watched it unmoving
deliberately on the bare floorboards he stepped up to
   Keating
Raised arms no protection against the messenger's
   crowbar.

Immeasurable strength in the quietness; the dulled
    hacking of iron:
smashed him in his grease-spotted clothes, arms,
    egg-head and shoulders
And without drawing breath he smashed Power and
    Mooney:
Whispered 'They sent me for you, so they did' with a
    simper
'But I had not gone for to crackle the jug.'

How to lay a mine

You clear the shallow earth away
bring your long rock-drill to the rock
and all morning long you beat it down while
the steel of its head and the steel of your sledge flow
    flakes, grows burning hot
and your mate the shaker perpetually turns the drill
From time to time he pours water down and brings up
    the dust
in the form of grey mud
and from time to time the drill jams but these are details.
At last the hole is deep enough
You take a stick of dynamite a malleable sausage of
    dynamite
thrust a long capped fuse into its body
and so right down the hole
followed by others, tamped carefully home
carefully, since at this point the future is uncertain and
    a spark
may scatter you and the shaker abroad
Earth over all, tamped harder still
the end of the fuse left free, an odd black stalk in the
    bareness
You fray the tip, set light to it, and as the sparks fly free
hissing, you walk off to watch the smoke at a distance.
There is no going back: it is all inevitable now, even
if a child or a chalice were sitting on the mine.
The smoke vanishes for now the flame bores underground
and the future is determinate: a false future, a kind of
    bastard present.
But the present is not with you yet

past and future confused and still this silence.
The earth leaps, rocks hurtle up black against the sky
a deadly hail of stone comes beating down
in the same moment you hear the boom of the explosion
smoke drifts from the gaping hole
present and future join; time runs orderly again.

The far side of the pass

On the far side of the pass it was still night
old night
but on this side it was the first of dawn:
even down there in the smooth sweeping valley
with its stream in the middle
there was dawn.
And in this pure innocent light all manner of creatures
were running
sheep from the mountain of course
and cattle below, with some ponies,
hens, and over to the right a small flock of guinea-fowl,
all running in a general far-away cheerful noise.
But what struck me stock-still, looking over and down
was those of the darkness itself
bloodsucking stoats weasels polecats
elegant careless lamb-killing foxes several badgers
bounding heavily, showing their joy by extravagant leaps
and many more martens than I thought the mountain
    could ever have held
splendid martens that glowed in the dawn.
And all these creatures were hurrying running streaming
    together
towards a sun that had never risen before.

August, Sun-impaled

A blazing strand
stones too hot to walk upon and
no refreshment in the milkwarm sea.
You lie there, seeing the red tide through your eyelids
nothing more
feeling the sun dissolve your fibre, bore right through
you lie there
hearing nothing but the waves
the crash and then
the long hissing grond of withdrawing surf
and silence once again.
The last wave might be like that
surcease surgecease
a last wave to a warm pink sightless world
no midnight: nor no pain.

Words from the bottom of a river

The Test, broad on this lower stretch and placid
too, except for the fall of weirs with deep holes
   under them:
broad and placid, clear as gin, the surface
almost completely flat.
And beneath the surface green perfect beds of weed
all facing one way quietly waving and between the beds
perfect gravel lanes: trout cruising in the lanes, feeding
   on pale watery nymphs.
High over, an enormous evening sky
violet, with architectural clouds.
Rounded banks, hay-high grass behind them
the occasional willow-tree.
landscape cows: church steeples, towers
A kingfisher, the blue streak of its flight
the red of its turn on seeing a woman:
she standing by the only muddy pool in the river,
a backwater with lilies
the broad leaves of lilies: there were bags there too
plastic bags and the limp evidence of cautious love
but what she gazed at were the bubbles
amorphous great lumps of air clumsily bursting,
   blurting upwards
bursting among the lilies so that they rocked conveying
   almost no meaning
Yet in time she made out the inept communication

   Be kind, my dear, I love you so
   I love you so be kind to me

Too late my friend she said aloud
and anyhow she added gently to herself
we meant quite different things
entirely different things you know.

Croagh Patrick

Pilgrims coming from the west side
turn by the gable of a tall grey house and begin
   their ascent.
it is a pity they should have left so many bottles:
the old boots and shoes are another matter entirely
for many make the climb barefoot
some even perform the stations on their knees
bleeding on the harsh scree.
I had not promised to make any stations
nor any circuits
only to reach the top
and even that I failed in.
Panting I gazed at the top and the torn sky over it
neither a great way from me
and oppressed by mundane obligations – by a
   dinner, no less –
I bowed, made my respects my excuses, turned
and at that very moment hail drove from the clouds
whipping my ears red and the rain soaked my jacket
as I ran leaping down with long skimming strides
followed me down, rights the way down
till I crossed the road itself to a chapel
a small roofless chapel where the O'Malleys bury:
and there in a niche behind were the altar had been
sitting easy, out of the weather, a chough
a red-billed red-legged black chough, shining with health
said 'There's a saint knows his own mind, I believe.'

A T'ang Landscape Remembered

Mists after mountain rain
Sun slanting through the pines that cling
to the walls of this
improbable chasm.
Feathery waterfalls drifting:
the unseen river sends up another mist of spray
It is all much the same, even to the twisted pine-tree over-
head and the feeling of detached unearthly height.

In this remembered landscape
only the sage is missing, the ancient happy man
leaning on a staff. The ancient man (obedient ears
attained long since) and his attendant boy.

I fill that place upon the mountain-path.
I do not fill it well: I have
no visible companions, no staff;
and when I bend, the face that stares back from the
     pool dismayed
has nothing of his wisdom: no trace of happiness.

Song

I had never supposed green eyes had charms
nor a musical tongue to be coming from Cork
until that I lay in my green love's arms
Poll Parrot cry havoc and ware the hawk
hoick Ranter, yoick Ranter, con tarran the hawk.

Farewell, my sin, I have enjoyed you

Food, drink and women:
there are chains.
Possessions, too.
Why add a strong, insistent, masterful
and new?

Smoke
good mornings' gate
forerunner, end and crown of meals
or hunger's stay
calm adjutant of peace and talk
first sign of manhood: in old age
a last delight.
Oh yes. All these and more.
No doubt the helot's very gay, though bound.

But over all
the principall.
Must smoke. an order Diktat ukase must
I do not like imperatives.

Besides
I throw
the arc of shooting stars, and hiss
it's gone.   Farewell
Farewell, my sin
    Goodbye

A *man under his impulsion*

Hurrying through the streams of grey, upslanting people
the desperate hunting through the insubstantial streets
those twilight cliffs of grey, vague buildings. pale
and crowded, colourless.
He incandescent; and alone
enclosed and silent, hunting and alone.

David danced before the ark

The unexpected patch of brown, the ploughland
in the valley; two furlongs up the valley from my window
squares in a naked wilderness of curve
and order spread on chaos
a handkerchief of order spread on chaos
   (four acres there in Scellog; oh a patch
   on this great naked sweeping valley)
Robert Roberts –
the ash tree's
moving branches
spoil my vision (naked twigs and branches still)
Yes it's Taid, the old man, Taid
a fine old strong one and is thick like oak.
But going strangely.
Stepping
He is stepping down the length of plough
a formal step, undeviating
Held straight and high: a backward leaning.
and head held high
His feet raise strangely; high and strangely, slow.

One his hand and two his hand
to the seed-bags – white the pouches
out and there the falling arc
flashing bow the falling seed
the momentary curve and shining
pulsing up and curve the curving
one half down the next is flying
and still renewed the pulsing fountain.
Oh blind the feet, the measured pacing

solemn, dedicated pacing
The high proud head, closed, half-unseeing
stern in the slow
the ancient ritual
solitary silent dance and holy
The priest
upon
his god's own body

The falling of the leaves

Sink. down in the grey sea
slowly down. The layers
silent of depression. down.
through thém.
No irritation, anger left
of red no hint
all only grey and silence welling
grey silent depths.
You sink your head
Down. breathing slow
Down eyes unfocussed staring
One tear creeps down the bent
ash dying face.

Dear Mona FitzPatrick '32 (or '3)

A boy – a man – I loved in County Down.
In the evenings, the sweet dusk of that summer
I used to turn my face to the North
writing writing and counting the days for a letter
(I was a boy)
longing the days long, my hands out to Ulster
I stood in the secret dark of the evening.

And now, on the evening path of a mountain, unthinking
it came fresh again:
familiar, familiar the sadness pervading
heart-worn the prayer for a wind from the north.

The theft

Hard running
feet running
flap, flap-flap, flap
and breaking-heart running
in the empty street.

The electric light failing

The town takes on its antique darkness
and in the streets, stumbling over the uneven cobbles
one sees the rooms lit with another light,
a light nearer the ground, more personal.
And the candle, the single candle gives a new meaning
    to the rooms inside the bead curtains
an ancient, unremembered focus.
Faces: hands: and a vast penumbra
in the living shadow hang shining pans – irrelevant
In the shade, more shadows on the shadows, moving
But above all, faces – the expressions clear-cut, intensified:
And the moving hands.

Youth gone

My youth
'the golden' as they say
(though brassy mine)
has slid away.

I still feel young
– at least, paray:
but looking now
my head is gray.

Giving up smoking

Virtue's self, I have not yet
smoked my morning cigarette.

Resolution wearing thin,
Driven down, impelled by sin
and hunger like a wolf within

To the shop, myself deriding
This my ninety-first backsliding.

Diego

Your workman, the one with the pulley on Thursday –
he's not a Frenchman?
Diego? No, said the mason
dust showing his trade, white powdering dust on his
    coat, in his gestures
dust flying and dust in his Pernod.
Diego's a Spaniard.

I like him, I said – had thought he was simple
Or deaf
He just shook his head when I spoke in the morning
But a good man, surely?
his worn face in mind, high-nosed and kindly
Ordinary, may be, but a good face, and lean.
The devil sucks fat men: the lean go to God.

He's poor, said Olifa, a gesture
showing the depth of the poverty
Never a word of a language but Spanish.
Scratching and pushing the cap off his forehead
Down there, he said, nodding,
He suffered.
Like others,
he fought and he suffered.

In the finish they took him
black jack-boots, revolvers, they took him
and numbered the soldiers whose turn was
for killing.
At dawn, the authoritarian dawn and grey

(precise for punctilio)
they came down the corridor
An unshaven sergeant, bunged-up and dirty
fixed irons on his hands.

Boots in the corridor
a file of men marching.
Loaded.
and all for Diego.

In the gateway
the thin light:
Diego
stared at the sky.
The sergeant gaped, staring upwards
Diego
ran ran and ran.
There was death on his shoulders.

They missed him, all missed him
no heart for the running and he out ahead
ran with the strength of the dead on his shoulders
speeding him out in the grey of the streets.
Grey streets, empty, and glistening tramlines
wide open streets, and as dead as the moon.
And one man, a small one, running in manacles.

A fortnight
in water
a dark hulk in the water

For fourteen days he ate nothing, Diego.
And his wife was in labour – he knew it
had numbered the days
starving in labour in the rat-trap they lived in.

Then to the mountains, high to Figueras
driving and forcing his legs to obey him
swollen and morbid, betraying Diego
But he draggled them over Arroja, the frontier.

What then? face at asking.
Why then, said the mason
down to Cerbère,
working: groping his way,
from Cerbère to this place,
and here a new woman
three children by her, and work in the fishing:
that's all.

Spaniards exiled

A woman singing
and in the narrow street the sun's hard shadows
straight hard-ruled shadows.
The unseen singing
ah the dying fall
the falling quaver of a Spanish song
querido, mi corazón.

They are often singing here, the Spanish people
in a far land strangers: they may not return
in a stranger's country and may not return.

The Captain and the Stock

Among the blacks the blue sea-captain stood
the fetish ground bare where the mangroves grew
(he had seduced the blacks with rum)
impatient now, the baptist much confirmed,
No lib for talk, says he, him stock and stone indeed.
Oh yes, him dash palabra, fetisso
they all replied and said, It would speak presently
they said, That they were very much surprised that it
    had not already responded, or replied.
In two hours he grew angry – the heat and flies
the damp sodden heat from the walls of the clearing
but the black men sat waiting and waiting for ever.
Steps to his feet and growls, disappointed
(was it not an illogical anger?)
If it is speaking, I am making it speak
the despicable pagan my cane to its gob
and he stabbed with his cane, a clouded Malacca
ungracefully lunged, a seafaring gesture
the pursed little mouth just round for the ferule
but the black men, dumbthundered, desired he would stop
dull leadish their faces, they wishes him to stop
standing just off the circle, they prayed him to stop
for the sake of his spirit they told him Forbear
Iconoclast captain, we beg you, forbear.
But a pair of small pistols, one primed in each pocket
by way of precaution in far foreign parts
or at home for that matter, for any surprise
point blank at the fetish and one for your nob
(warmed now by his fervour) But never a word.
There, I knew it was idle: I said so before.

returned to his cabin
If it <u>could</u> have spoke, then was the time
the ill-favoured image
it certainly would have, the moment I shot it
but I knew that it was only a stock of wood, and
   impossible that it should speak
ever.
And so he repeated, the days of his life
repeated repeated forgetting by story
repeating repeating forgot in the telling
the smell of the mangroves
the tropical land
far, far: far
the words through the years
not the thing
until he was sitting, deaf now and thin blooded
and sitting alone, in the cold Coetmor
the now-scattered stones (evil stones) Coetmor
the silent and ancient oh cold Coetmor
it came to him then.

To *the hermitage and down, refreshed*

I went up to the Consolation
Notre-Dame de la Consolation –
they call the place the Consolation
Up through the town, the faubourg
railway bridge, the fork
and from the houses up
past the olives and
the cork-oak grove
the bridge
(though dry)
The vines and little boxes all the way
white shrines
and withered bunches through the bars
What saints? Saint Anne for one
And up
the path is narrow
to the trees
a hollow with the noble chestnut trees
the hermitage
commercialised? I see a bar
and smell the radical republican
                              republican the publican

Yoho the key
and ho the key
the long-legg'd child
gives me the key
the long shanked key
and heavy key
and very heavy long old key

Turn and I open, what is here?
No desecration here.
Now good, and unexpected: bless them too:
The alter, candles and an eikon (stranger here)
Saints plain and coloured.
And in boxes Ships
Oh see the ships
the rigging, sails, the waves, the sea
A dark explosion here and bloody wreck
the sailor's presents from the doubtful sea.
Above the aisle
a crocodile
a stuffed malignant
crocodile.
But on the pillars, on the whitewashed walls
graffiti.
Low by the floor, up high as hands can reach
no place without a scribbled thing.
What to expect? Names, dates and hearts
the names of towns, obscenity?
the things they write on every goddam wall
in Notre-Dame in Paris and in Pompeii?
For once the worst is wrong, and this one runs
    Holy Virgin
    make him love me
    make the one I love love me

    Health in sickness
    Health from sickness
    freedom from the failing sickness

Freedom for our men, Madonna
Stalag Ten in Würtemburg
The bitter years mount fast between us
Give us back the men we love.

Waiting for money in a far country

No, they said at the post, there is nothing. There is
    nothing for that name.
The satisfied shaking head far clearer than the words
and the dull black haired woman protected by a grill
    was glad that there was nothing
the yellow face under the dull hair, and notices forbidding.
Out, and the heat by the bull-ring: the glare and the
    unceasing rush of the hot wind
the hard dry heartless yuccas and the wind
no air in the wind: dust and the perpetual rushing of
    the wind.
the passport back in the pocket – sweat from the small
    effort, for the corners stick.
How many days to London? Allow the week-end desert
One to answer – it is urgent they will write at once –
    and so many back.
How much money? Count one two three
money as filthy as the by-word: dirty, dirty paper.
Divide. Can it be done? It must be done and must be done
but what if they ask for their money?
Gall in the stomach.
Have the letters gone to the wrong address, astray in Paris?
It was madness to let the money go so fast; so low now.
A wire?
And see the long thin envelope tomorrow, look a fool,
    and poor?
Shame stands before the door: one cannot ask again
shame can kill men die of shame
Not till tomorrow.
Kill the time and murder it read a book and murder that.

No sleep.
The wind for ever and the flies
no sleep, but dreams of telegrams in montage – palimpsests,
counting and dividing.
Dare one go and see? The queuing for the words to
    sear the day and all those plans
so frail they are now – all is spent and all must wreck.
Better have hope today: avoid them on the stairs, go
    south about
it's sure tonight. Four days and one for chance
And sure it is indeed.

But not tonight, nor any other night
and accidie shall wait on fifty pound.

On the broad green desk, baskets In and Out.
These only want your signing – contracts, cheques.
This fellow. yes. Annoyed me at the Ivy – talked too much

no, said Barabbas, he can wait.

In Madame Ponsalié's garden

Green bronze oranges round and hard on the thick branches
and the long cones of unexpected green thorns to them,
   yellow-tipped
Slips, scions, grafts.
The little sort of pick-axe.
Dead brown flaccid pears by the wall and over the wall
   the improbable burst of a palm, with a dark strong
   magnolia this side of it.
A dove. And the satisfying ringing click of billiard balls.
In that very French high-slanting slate-roofed house
   they are playing billiards.
But on the right there is a proper roof – rose tiles,
   half round
and behind that roof the far liquid notes of a piano:
   unrelated because of the wind.
Here it is calm and the leaves fall with a dry rustle,
   when they fall, severally.
A rose, thorns and an unlikely red standing there in the
   bare trodden earth.
At the bottom, rabbits in boxes – a deep couch of dung.
A dung-hill, but inoffensive: and a gourd. No melon; I
   think a gourd.
It is round on the bare earth.
Down the middle the path and the orange trees
on the far side daisies, yellow, high, many-headed,
   and weeds
unknown bushes, and stretching I see another palm, by
   the iron gate
the squat thick trunk, can it be right, the wood?
In front distant cries – French, those

Behind, unseen black ancient tiny women, and the
harder Catalan.
The dove again, and over the deep sky, clouds from the
north-west

Walk by the sea to see wonders

On the edge of the sea, no stir
the sand is dry;
on the rocks, no foam.
No fan in the air, and the high mist hangs
a veil on the sky.
Smooth beyond calmness, the sea
has lost its sea-nature:
unnatural; soft.
inverted – the fish-view.

Fresh-fallen, luminous snow
vast wastes of it, high
is akin to this sea
But here there are colours
the light and God's colours
oh Sea: oh nacreous sea.

    And there, to prove the ancients right
    the long blue flash, the halcyon's flight.
    Upon the sea?
    That cannot be.
    But there, upon the rock, are three.

And round the edge a streak of cloud
brown, far darker than the sea
straight, unvaried misty cloud
but the sea is softer than the cloud
far softer than the softest cloud.
The boats stand spaced upon the sea
spaced in the silver of a glass –

the silver of the water's skin
seen from below, ephanides
the meaning's clear? Be damned to these
half-meaning laboured similes
There was the calm of heaven there
the peace of God beyond compare.

The raven

The raven of the Pyrenees
cries Aark and folds his wings to fall
On Moelwyn Mawr the watcher sees
the raven tumble, and the call
the deep harsh Aark, he hears the call.

The young listless man

The burden of life too young
he had broken underneath it.
too young.
I saw
the loud-mouthed slut that he had married
(quick and regretting as he married)
big-bellied year by year
A dirty whining trail of children
oppressed neglected ugly children
a sordid, cold, a squalid kitchen;
and cigarettes at three and four.
If he had been a man and growen
a hard-backed man and strong beside
he might have stood and worked to greyness
and fought his life and won his pride:
But he was just a boy, a soft one
and it had crushed him flat, unknowing.
and flat; unknowing.

From the Welsh

The wood of birds
wind singing in the wood of birds
and sun green in the leaves, young leaves.
But bowed and crouching on the moss
the sun-warmed stones by Coed Tŷ
eyes staring sightless on the ground
I sat enveloping my pain
the pain the pain oh God the pain
the tearing pain, there in my heart.

Snowdon for the sunrise

In the dark of the night before the moon rose they
    went down the worn road
it showed white, faint in the darkness
and the dogs, before and behind, were momentary
    shadows on the darkness.
Turn at the groeslon and up through the stark
    silent village
(cold even now the warm night time, stark cold
    in its lines)
delicately walking but their iron heels clattered and the
    iron gate clashed by the chapel
a dog – but the dogs knew them.
Now steep climbing the ancient road, loose shale and
    rocks up through the dwarf oak and the hazels
up and to the smooth turf on the ridge
warm and the smooth turf. No wind.
On the far left the vague plain of the distant sea
and on the right the stab of Cnicht
a thin dark dagger lance triangle stabbing the darker sky
before, a nothing, an obscurity
and in it Snowdon. Long miles between, and the road's
    long twisting.
Not midnight yet.

Down; the rock Ben-gam, and there
the standing pools of mist
sweet-gale, and the moving of a bird
the drifting scent of sweet-gale
and below, still there below
Cae Ddafydd, and the hurring

half-heard gentle fern-owl
nightjar hurring through and through
the honied warmth and dark caressing night.

The wine-dark sea

The 'wine-dark sea' a commonplace?
Poetic argot's hollow ring?
It is not so, I know, to me
who saw last night the purple sea
the even, gently-swelling sea
unbroken, smooth and menacing.

The purple with an edge of blue,
And reddish in the after-glow
the spindrift floating on the waves:
The foaming, dark and rasping wine
they trod in vats some months ago –
These were the same. But then the moon
rose to the edge and spoilt the sea's
wine-dark dove's bosom: over these
the nascent stars; Aldebaran
and, half unseen, the Pleiades.

The bad day

Mad women, talking inwards, crazed, and
crippled men, deformed (erased red eyes, half blind)
and evil tongues
All in rusty black in black shawls
and black stockings in the white flare flaming sun
There in the shadow of the rococo church
the yellow greasy preez
is creeping from his Mass – black, whatever
   he may say.

Sterne

A red haired head with close-set shallow eyes
a glabrous, pimpled face and yellow teeth
clothes dirty black
but fleshy whitish hands, moist, fidgeting
They open and they close, the unctuous palms.
A pen still itching, and it runs
On God and testicles: the ink is slime.
The furtive eyes are ready with a leer,
must share the leachery; he paws you, breathing close
'How is your pulse now, madam?'
And then the pumped-up sob; the little eyes have tears.

But these same eyes, turned inwards from the asterisk
See Uncle Toby and the upright Corporal Trim.

The Pleiades on Christmas Eve

O see the shiners
six I see
right overhead (the Christmas tree)
they make a jewel
but not for me
the misty stars are not for me

but if they were
O then I say
　　(and wrapped in cloud
　　　　　　　　for holiday)
then I should have
should have my way
and you a gift
for Christmas Day.

The apology

She asked me did I love her
and I
made dumb by old abuse
made no reply.

A word so used, so greasy with the using
crooned, trumpeted out, the lush
forerunner of the furtive pox
among the dregs
And by me
in far-off sordid grapples
– another self, but still the mouth's the same mouth's
    shame the same
And that alas O harrow and alas. But no help now:
    blind face it is.
Is that to be
the word
t'apply
to this deep unity?

On the left a half-paid, old, unsmiling whore
whose grin does not conceal a mind averse
And here, the one sole thing the sole one thing that
    gives to death

a terrible finality, a fear
of loss unmeasured: makes of it the sum
of all the bitter tearing wind of sorrow
man can feel.
The wheel

on which he breaks
quite breaks
Breaks.
Down. He is down.
Breaks quite down. Smashed now –
never and never and never and never again
this whole man now.

Do these two meet?

Dead hours of louring justification,
a desert of time

With ash on your love
you are dying in little
with grey ash on your
love, you fool.

Myself a young man read a poem

I was young and read a poem
Timor mortis conturbat me;
The first real mortal knowledge, understanding
how deep it bit, the biting
surety of coming death for me.

Death for others – theoretic. By all means death for
   them
the natural order, death for them
the old and barely human.
Death-bed, 'fell asleep', the service
orderly and regular
and quite unreal.
This
changed suddenly to waiting
a trapped and hopeless waiting.

From a to x (an x with limits)
a shining dot, the present figured,
rushing on to x's zone
the length or shortness relative
and almost unimportant now.
Waiting in a waiting room.
With years it darkened
twice the number, square the sum
twice the loss, a double waiting.
the x's do not coincide.
Death to break us from each other
holding, holding to our love
Death by night, death in the morning

Death tomorrow in the sun.
I wished I had not read the poem
the face had been the same, but so
I wished I had not read the poem.

Now with years, and death much nearer
its power has gone. gone
diminished, dwindled, far receded
A true proportion?
is it?
to grip the present, live it
not smash your head against the wall?

The uncertain land

He had dispossessed them of their land
the patient laborious people.
The agent had looked to the sordid work – was paid
    for the sordid work
the letters writs eviction.
So they lived in the bog now, with the piled turf for a wall
and brushwood for their habitation.
And he walked with clean hands on their land
with his soft buttoned leggings
and his Purdy under his oxter – the obedient unloving
    dog at his heels.
Where there was a dry whisp on the bog
was a snipe, or a cock in the bushes
And the man and his people hid there in the bushes
they were trespassers now on their land.
They wished him the heart-searing curse, the black
    curse of God on his soul
the priest's curse and the torturing death to his soul
The dark hate flowed out from the shadows, the
    bushes, and he unaware.
Smirking and princing there in the open.
with his little sandy moustache, smooth pink complacency
the evil man walked in the sun, the sun darkened.
In the middle the elegant green of the emerald
a bubble of turf
the rain made these bubbles when it fell on Kilanna.
Sin on two legs, he walked to the bubble
Its edges were cushions – or fleshy? They quivered
Flesh he said in his personal ear, and stepped
    to the middle

The thing heaved – a jelly and flesh under the green
The conceit made him snigger – the earth's heaving belly.
In the middle he stood and danced on his feet
heavy and apish capering alone in the open
and his pendulous lip flabbed as he jumped.
With his knees bent and his legs apart
he jumped and it heaved, the yielding the pleasure
and the third leap it gave, the green mat the traitor
the fibres tore under him, a door to the blackness
through to the blackness, the soft mud, thin, stinking.
No foothold
his hands scrabbled the rushes
tore-clawed them, they giving the traitors
Down and no foothold
sweat washing the
smirk off his face
Down and no foothold
toes searching, no foothold
and under his arms the grass tearing in gobbets
impotent claws
on the unhelping thin slivers
and unctuous the slivers
There was no help below him.
Down and no help for him. On the whole of the earth
there was no help to sustain him.
His agony died in the mud of Kilanna
and his agony pleased the laborious people
it laid warmth to the hearts of the patient laborious
    people.
His gun lay clean aside on the rushes

and seeing the black of the hole had done stirring
the unloving dog stood
and turned to rove for its pleasure.

Silver-haired charm and urbanity

Inventing, she added a pinch to the mixture
finger and thumb to the aniseed box
O very delightful said the household of people
eating them quickly.
These cakes are delightful.

Delighted, she put in a good ten, a dozen
swept clean the hearthstone and blew on the fire.
What the devil's the matter?
the anger, disaster
What the devil's the matter?
These cakes to the dog.

Weeping and weeping, the cakes on the flagstones
they were left and despised by the gluttonous dog
he could not endure them, the gluttonous dog.

Winter in Foreign Parts

The vines, the cork trees, olives and the thyme
tall cactuses, and sweet the mountain air,
the harsh dry polished rattle – palm fronds
in the breeze
all these
I had preposed.
But not the London sparrow, magpie, crow;
still less the stars by night, our Plough and Bear
the same Orion; Rigel, Altair there
and through the trees the shining Procyon.

Obsèques

Charmed to be carrying the Cross that boy
vacillating, gaping boy
the high and silver Cross comes first
(boys black and white, and edged with lace)
The priests:
the old, smooth, Roman face
and strong
(the people love him here – vrai bout de pain)
the other young and commonplace
complacent – o a vulgar lard –
talking: bends to old the bowed biretta
talks breathes and talks
quite loud.
A space. The horse
the ghastly knacker's nag, the horse
dull shambling before the hearse
the graveyard horse. the horse of paradise
The driver strangely out of place in working clothes
cloth cap and lounging there
is self possessed.
Flowers. And on the hearse's lid
deep, fingered, written dust.
A flood of men comes through the arch
by threes and fours: aligned
heads bowed and backward hands inclasped.
Some black (but rare), best blue, a uniform
the black in front.
Do they know gravity at all? Perhaps
but not outside
the urgent, vital need to talk, the public tongue

dumb piety is overlaid
you slouching, smirking cigarette, why come?
But here the women, here is grief indeed.
Oh grief upheld and tottering in weeds
full sail in veil, the relish of the day.
The stream flows black entirely now
black hundreds pass. No end?
Oh yes, the end: the lines grow thin
and colours coming now – those greening girls
and suddenly the end.
The high shrill talk is dying on the left
it is the end
but one old woman, hurrying
a boney, black-wrapped face and hurrying
to see the end.

The dark figures

On the left hand the sea
on the right are the mountains
On the right hand the high mountains
and a hill there with a castle upon it.

The strong light in the evening slanting
the golden summery light of the evening
showed a row of dark figures up there by the castle
I thought they were people regarding the castle
(too large, but distance is strange in the evening).
They were still there tomorrow,
strained and attentive, unchanging
On the ridge of the hill a row of small cypresses.

In the autumn I saw the row of dark figures
– a Thursday – but the wind from the mountains
had curved them; and bowing, the figures
were turned away from the castle.

They were bowing in harmony to the Mediterrarmony.

'Is *true the rat*'

A naturally embalmed rat on the shingle: probably from under the floor-boards of one of the larger fishing-boats.

Is true the rat
the alabaster, paper
rat
the wind would turn?
No hair on that. flat. rat.
Dirty-white and yellow. dry.
unnatural and yet
a perfect rat.
The type of rat.
Though centimetre flat and dried
the living evil in its face
is now intensified.

The duty of pleasure

You lie there unmoving
unreading, the dark of the shadow
squat indigo shadow
compressed by the weight of the
unbreathable air
you panting; oppressed and unhappy
pinned
by the unwinking, unmoving, inimical sun.

The dead air on the foreshore
dancing in fever (sick headache to look at)
destroying the bay.
and the waves curl slow
they sigh
and die
sigh on the shingle
withdrawing: a sigh and a pause so long
you think that the sea has tired
retired and died
pond
an ocean no more.

Poulp: or, the Medusa a Toy

The octopus: there is the beast of all creatures
for loathing and hatred.
The horror near retching of its swollen and boneless
uncoloured head
the calm steady pulsing of the valve in its head
in the seething malignance and writhe of its feelers
arms perpetually seeking, a tentacle entity.
And obscene fascination. A violence of feeling
as strong as a bull-fight.
Not unlike a bull-fight, the whole drained of colour,
no sound or perspective
or people: a bull-fight
with only the horror and long fascination.
Myself I have seen one
touched it and felt it,
It living
bloated potent and viscid malignance
and strong – strong with a strength to make shudder.
In the sunlight I stared at the creature, tide's captive
hours crouched in a silent
reluctant communion
looking into the unwavering eyes of the creature
a yellow implacable glaring: and lidless oh lidless.

Grey and white

This city afternoon,
Grey London, gruel-thin,
Sets gulls upon its river,
And half-mast pigeons float in Berkeley Square
The white and grey:
The half-tone chess
That no one ever played.
But see how the birds
Are buoyed in the grey air.

No smoking: the second day

Waking to the knowledge that I must not smoke
I next recalled our quarrel of the night
with all the bitter words that both sides spoke,
and anger made me take my pen and write:
    'I knew of old when love grew cold
    the common mould betrayed the scold;
    but thought that you, to rareness true,
    could not become a vulgar shrew.'
And pausing then to let the rhyme restart
And staring from my window to the street
I saw you pass, and all at once my heart
unclenched, unfolded, would no longer cheat,
refused to play the hateful act or write
the false, the hurting words, the wicked game:
my nerves, tobacco-starved, stretched jangling-tight,
sighed and relaxed; and blushing then for shame
I asked forgiveness, praying that you might,
Griselda-like, know whence the anger came
and might concede unto the weed
its rightful meed,
the burden of the blame.

Pray, Luv, forgive me my sourness

Think of me
no uncharity
But have in gree
My love for thee,

And account not my dourness.

For heavy cheer
And loutish leer
All loathly gear
Comes not near

Your P.

The Mandrake

She had not pulled a root, a root,
A root but barely five
When hellish shrieked the smallest shoot,
Says, Lady, I'm alive.
Oh see you not the blood he said
That purples me around,
Oh see you not the blood he said,
Lies darkling on the ground?

For I was once a man in deed
Where now I am a root
and underneath my seven leaves
I bear a forked root
A forked root that down does pierce
Unto the bones below
The skull, the breastbone and the ribs
That once my flesh did know.

And they have waited many years
These hundred score and nine
As do the bones of self-killed men
Yet still the bones are mine.
The worms have wasted all my heart
These long years were their gain,
Yet had the root but touched the rib
I'd grown it there again.

But you have plucked my root lady
Before it touched the bone
And you have spread my blood abroad

It dries there on the stone.
Oh had you left me but a day
A day but barely one,
The root had touched, and I had been
The mandrake's naked son.

But you have broke my seven leaves
And turned me back to hell:
Each leaf it was three hundred years
Oh Lady did you well?
And you have torn me from my grave
That was my cradle too
And for this thing that you have done
My curse shall make you rue
And when the moon is dark he said
And the sun's in agony
The nearest meat that ever you eat
Shall choke both your true love and you.

For Louise's visitors' book

Trees rising straight without the least transition
a woman tall and unexpected like the trees those
elegant and witty scented pines
terrace after terrace falling to the seas
two seas
the one hemmed in with castles jetties moles
a swarm of pink-roofed houses over there, boats
    swimming, bathers, sharks
domestic contemplative sea: but to the right
untouched the seven million waves to Africa.
Three hundred suns the tramontane
three hundred moons and Venus and the Pleiades
weave the year through the needles of the pines
the turning years the centuries.

'Clouds over clouds'

Clouds over clouds, building up from in back of the mountain. The door opened, the rain had stopped during the night. The wind cold from through the trees. Burned on the leaves, cold. Coming through the door and lifting the papers on the table. Brown.

Paper. Dolls. When she didn't go out.

Looking at the door through the draft in the light.

The leaves folding in. Around the trees. Blueish on the forest.

His face undone and packaged inside. Fitted behind, the sky tucked in the corners and around the outside. Pulled down tight and tied underneath.

She touched the clouds and the light from the other room.

Coming in doors.

Full.

She stood in front.

Her hands running over the leaves.

The rain had poured out the cheeks on the crest of the mountain.

The rock bone washed out pockets in the clothes hung on green.

Buried by the sun.

The light through the trees, shafts cut in the forest.

Her legs in the wind. Cold through the trees.

Unwrapped turning slowly the road around the side of the mountain. Where the light came into her eye. On the blue sky through the clouds a patch behind the mountain.

She cut forward through her eye. Through the fields.

The sun pulled along the length of the road on the shadows of the grass.

From the corner of his mouth, leaves.

In the weather from his eye spread on the sky she filled in the moon the clouds on the mountain the rain pulled out from the bottom fell on the fields. Flowers on the banks of his hand.

Ahead where she watched the road.

And waited.

'Walking on the high mountain'

Walking on the high mountain – the path
leading up into the dimness under the ridge.
Behind, the sea, an immeasurable disc. Lights far far below.
On either hand the lower hills, rounding down to the
   dark plain.
Remote. And I have come for the remoteness.
Yet here on the path there is the smell of thyme:
on the bare ground between the grass and the cistus
my torch lights up a badger's foot-mark.
The long-considered argument drops from me like a shroud
and in the torch-lit darkness
my heart is importuned by joy.

'Help my understanding, Lady'

Help my understanding, Lady
Books and numbers, books and school.
I cannot understand them, Lady
help me or I stay a fool.

  Distorted – well of course they are
  can't put the French: transfigured too
  Did you require a guide-book Sir?

Our Lady, help my father's sorrow
Please to help my father's sorrow.
Oh, Our Lady, please.

Please may I rise a form next term?
Or if I cannot rise a form
Please may I be the first in this
or second, third or fourth?

No ugly thing among them all
but altruistic love there is
(and 'love for others' oh the cant)
<u>and</u> love for others: that an't cant, the pure
and ancient ancient piety.

'Down through the vines'

Down through the vines, the changing vines
the grapes are gone, the changing vines
<u>One</u> of those writings clears the saints
outweighs the tinsel, ribbons, zinc
of everlasting awful flowers
the plaster hearts with stabbing thorns
the hymn in urchins' spines (with notes)

The crocodile and ships want no excuse.

Collioure

Upon a shallow bay the sun, the sacred phallus
and the rows
rose rows of planes tip-tilted in the sun
harsh angled shadows, rigid violet shade
and cactuses.
O cactuses, the Catalans
the spiny, crowded Catalans
their hands, they spread their palmate hands
roast, frozen, baked: the shallow soil
an ancient, bitter shallow soil
sustains, but just sustains their roots
resentfully sustains their roots.
Their god for ever is the sun. He kills
and feeds them: holy sun.
Their hands for ever to the sun.
Inimical, the cactuses
with spines hard eager in their hands
this land, this acrid land is theirs
You want to share the sterile land?
Old, savage, worn, resenting land?
And worship too?
No room: the thorns are close
and closer close the crowded hands
Yet in the thorns you see a fruit
a strange, a living, crimson fruit
the sun-engendered blazing fruit
and
The matrix of the Catalans

'Long, straight, the steel lines'

Long, straight, the steel lines
the railed way perpetually vanishing in perspective
Narbonne, Carcassonne, Toulouse.
The middle parts of France; an unending road
unwinding, like a film
Such distances: so many trees.
And even then the sea
(A poor sort of broad public nuisance full of orange peel
And bounded by dingy sheds)
before the right true end
So much mere space, confused by winds in darkness, noise,
between this sky and that
between the silver olives and the Hyde Park elms:
the loudest voice can scarcely shout a message through –
the meaning of the words is lost.
Strange echoes, the timbre of other rooms, the angling
of all the intervening bells.

'If I could go back into my dream'

If I could go back into my dream
I should see the cheetahs again & the leopards &
   the unknown
sharp-faced brute in the abandoned houses off Pall Mall
And I should know those sharp exactly-pointed things I
   said (& wrote)
      for 1 dream was also there in print-transparencies.
Which stripped off all the wool & fuzz
from what burns down at a layer beyond common words
the heart of the matter, which beats deeper than the
   reach of usual words,
How it floats beyond my groping
Intangible except for meaningless haphazard points
unrecognized until you meet it bang
running head-on round a corner in a street
inhabited by independent polar bears
And suddenly you know that this is it
Of course: the plain, self evident essential truth.

'Loose-bellied, grey'

Loose-bellied, grey, cross, absolute,
I am eroded by success
and failure eats away my heart
The things that fill the years have drunk
my heart's blood, leaving it quite dry.

Old Men

We are old bald ugly
impotent and fat or horribly lean
unarmed disarmed often unspeakably silly
Nobody wants us
least of all ourselves

Our wives are short thick and spectacled
with elaborate hair
nobody wants them
least of all ourselves

It is a crime against humanity
that old people
racked with ignominies, weak
should be made to pay pay pay
and then pay
for a life that has already been lived

'When your lance fails'

When your lance fails
When your lance fails
When your lance
fails
you must dismount forever
and join the ludicrous ranks
of the old contemptibles
waiting for death
with what fortitude they can assume.
& if you can do so without crying out it is too soon it is
not fair you are a better man than I am capon dear.

Part II: Drafts

The Sardana for the First Time

In the <u>Place</u>, naked lights hang in the trees,
the leaves by them an unnatural brilliant green.
Below, are lines of people, a square.
People lining the Place.
The front row sits on the warm paving stones – the warmth
rises in the evening and the stones are soft
and there are benches. Behind, the others stand,
some lean in doorways
They are waiting the Sardana.
Now the harsh tense unexpected screaming of a single pipe
before the music
and then the music. Loud discordancy
Barbarous to an unaccustomed ear
unnatural intervals and time
a harsh high braying, crude, unripe.
No easy sweetness; here no pretty trilling ditty
and thump, the nagging beat, irregular, unmeaning –
But not to them.
the first men stand out in the open
just stand there, quite indifferent. Some old, some young
and now three girls. Join hands, a ring
but hardly move.
And over them and through the trees the crying spate of
sound.
An undetected change in rhythm and the dance begins.
Small life, dull shuffled paces and the faces grave
some faces grave, some talking, grinning – jokes
but soon are grave and priestlike – hieratic is the word – and
firm.
Of course the music and the dance are one

dull clod. I was those minute-years ago (but richer now)
The rhythm stops
a brutal thump. No more.
The hands go downwards, centripetal in
a hand quick shake and now the pattern breaks
the fragments insignificant – a shopman or a sardine factory
hand
No longer priests
The darkness and the shining trees are different now,
anticlimax, detumescence now
a flat awakening
How far you were removed
Up and high-pierced, saturated with the music, rapt.
Relaxed now
but still unsatisfied and hungry for the next
waiting for the single pipe again
Wait long and hard and here it is again
harsh shrill stab right to the middle ear
a jet of brittle sound and longed-for pain.

'Yesterday an old husband'

Yesterday an old husband
saw his boyhood fairing thrown out
much worn often repaired but not beyond repair
even from the utilitarian point of view
Today he hangs not indeed himself from the rafter
but a quantity of salt perhaps disproportionate
the crack of a ball against a coconut the triumphant turn
and takes down a little more old sour resentment.

'Whereas in Jewry came a star'

Whereas in Jewry came a star
And was a ferly sight
The ass was tied to the stable barn
Right close by Mary bright.
And when the star was overhead
And then three Kings came also
And Joseph stood by the lowly bed
And the Kings knelt all in a row
Then all the beasts within the stall
Deo gratias loud did say
But for the little gentle ass
Who nothing could but bray.

Now hold thy peace thou tender beast
Old Joseph he can say
And hold thy peace, whereas thou feast
On this first Christmas Day.
Thereat the ass hung down his head
To do what he was bade
Though he were fairer to have said
Somewhat both blithe and glad.

'Not that a hard-roed herring should presume'

Not that a hard-roed herring should presume
To swing the tithe-pig in a catskin purse;
Nor fear the hail-stones that may fall in Rome
By lessening of their fall to make it worse.
And then the evil that so far from home
Portends the failure of the judgment-seat
The rank strong fires of democratic rule
Subverts the ancient order to repeat
Moon-pall. moon-pall. moon-pall
Methusalem.

'The pattering of rain'

The pattering of rain
heavy drops falling from the chestnut trees
The garden bowed under the sodden sky
Water running gently onto the gravel
The double lines of the gravel drive
The basement windows of the palace
look into a confusion of papers, bags, scribbled notes,
    the telephone
a huge indomitable old woman
lying nestled in confusion.
High in the library of apparent books
and a girl, still lovely in her moments,
the uneaten half resisting
confused in love duty hatred
burns inevitably away.

'The cry of buzzards in the sky'

The cry of buzzards in the sky
beaks touching, kissing in the sky
and lost to view on Moelwyn Mawr.
Two ravens on their single road
straight-flying on the straight-ruled road
and talking through a mile of air.
The brushing steady beat of wings
the pulsing on the silent air.
The scent of green.
The croziers of form; and double shouting,
   drunk and shouting
hoarse cuckoos playing on the Braich y Parc.

The grey sheep scatter: there the line of white
the climbing working line of hounds
intent and working through the scree
high on the shoulder of the Do'aean Fawr
They hit the drag and silent Lliwedd rings
the savage echo of a cry of hounds.

'Vicious intromission'

Vicious intromission is a legal term
As children we played at coach and horses
The stabbing of inwit steady and firm
Is (by far) the most sterile of all known moral forces.
By far.

Forbear O Venus pray forbear

Forbear O Venus pray forbear I read
in Horace many years ago
Desine saeva Venus precor
(Or have I got it wrong?)
And wondered much that he should fear
the pangs that then I longed to know
The glowing dart that draws the tear
of dear delight, the honeyed flow
of love's unending interchange
(whatever that may mean) & those
~~ideas were all confirmed by my authorities~~.

A *halt* on the Trans-Siberian

A Tartar cleared the table, drank up the madeira sauce
hooking it with an ancient finger:
stared at the electric fire
bemused by years by waiting in a restaurant by
    all these languages
by Old Believers, protopopes
Lenin Stalin Stenka Razin and now
tourists: by this electric fire.
The Obu sturgeon had become a megawatt
tourists came to view this megawatt.
The megawatt became the fire, the fire a steppe:
tall summer grass, wormwood, a crimson river. Tartar
    horses on the steppe
and stretching up his scrawny neck he screeched
    and boomed
deeper than a bittern, sang:
Thick, the white horse's mane
Thick, thick, the white horse's mane.
I shall make a raft on the flowing river
If my cords cannot hold the raft I must
yield up my head to servitude.
Where the salt-flowers grind under foot
the stallion and the mare stand on far-separated banks:
the tall brother and the short brother
lurk about the Voivode's gate.

'When my Muse and Chian Veins vie'

When my Muse and Chian Veins vie
For which shall have the mastery
Than am I sorely vexed
And woefully perplexed
For the one without the other's dull
And t'other sans the one's a trull
Yet will they not combine
The bull yearns still for kine
And the Muse lies crimson coy
Loathing that she should enjoy
Alas, out harrow and alas
That love should go in the shape of an ass

The sorrow & woe

To bed with slow acid dripping toward one's head:
blameworthy, pull for cowardly, and soon escape
and out of the mist of chemical ill-tasting stupor
– still far we carry: and yet dawn –
rising up, the memory of yesterday and
its gratuitous barren unhappiness.

Boars

Up and up, perpetually climbing, up
past the half-dead villages and up the bush-grown road
through the four deserted hamlets
beyond them and the last roofless farms
beyond all tracks and ancient deep-worn lanes
high into the mountain, fold after fold
and every fold rising higher, vaster still, sloping to the sky.
Forest nearly all of it, though sparse at times
and now and then a precipice, a waterfall.
From dawn the young man had been climbing up
a fine springing stride as though he meant
to pass, an urgent refugee, across the frontier into Spain:
he was in fact moved fast by love and by the love
of those precious mushrooms, bolets, cèpes, that moved
    all the people that he lived among
when autumn came – love, love of the mountain and
    the mountain's cèpes.
Although he was a townsman now, tending a machine
    with forty-seven wheels
his blood moved with the seasons still:
and not his alone, for half the little town turned out
when the leaves fell and the scent of fungus wafted
    through the trees – he
had left Old Lard the grocer and his own foreman five
    miles back, gasping
on the graveyard-wall of ruined Saint Senen, where a
rusting notice told them to beware the trap for wolves.
Now he too paused and at a sudden crest, a grassy crest
leant his gun against an upright rock, sat on the turf,
    ate hard sausage wedged

into a loaf of bread, ate voraciously; squirted wine
    from a leather bottle,
leaning back his head.
And leaning back his head perceived an eagle in the sky
    the last
snake-eagle lingering into the fall, White John, an eagle
    of no great size
not much more than seven feet across and flying
    clumsily, flapping, agitated
for he too was dining – a serpent caught up from
    basking in the sun
inserted head-first and stuffed down inch by inch in
    spite of its rebellion.
A familiar sight, for the young man's grandfather had
    farmed Saint Senen:
his childhood had been filled with the scent of cows,
    the sharp piercing reek of pigs
never could be caught again.
The watch he gazed at conveyed anxiety rather than the
    time of day
he could not tell the time in fact – relied on hooters,
    bells – nor
for that matter could he really read.
You will never prove a phoenix, Martin, said the
    master of his school, how true.
Like the borrowed gun (a cruel burden to a mushroom-
    creeper)
the watch was there only to impress his love.
The sun a surer clock stated that it was too late
too late to make the round of Mala Cara.

The only hope of finding her and them was by the peak
   itself
straight up and over, cutting the valleys that lay
   between.
During this time the light had changed, and already he
   was well beyond
the familiar country of his childhood days: but the
   general lie seemed clear enough and
picking up the gun he plunged bald-headed down.
He crossed a stream
Climbed, plunged, and crossed another.
Again: the country stranger still. And now there was a
   meeting of the waters, two streams
coming from the right and left, and between them lay
a heart-shaped island, such a sward, a perfect sward all
   spotted with the finest cèpes
more than he had ever seen at once cèpes you would
   go ten miles to find.
But the sun was beneath the nearer ridge. He leapt
   straight across
the certain expectation fading to anxious hope no more,
   and that
uttering frequent cries to urge him on.
Running where he could, and scrambling fast, with time
   running faster still
sweat scratches gasping breath.
Clouds in the sky at last, what sky there was: for here
by a last stream barring an unknown coomb
the broad beeches stood so thick that there was little
   sky.

The mountains had changed shape; and he was lost.
He cooled his sad and disappointed face, splashing the
    yellow water on his neck;
and as he bent to cross he saw boars' tracks upon the
    bank
familiar half-moons pressed deep into the mud.
He had known them for ever, boars; and he had some-
    times heard or even seen the beasts themselves
dark shapes in the undergrowth when he was a little
    boy: but mostly dead
for in hard winter they would raid the farms by night
when he was five a strong band had rooted up
Turnips.
Potatoes
Yams.
In an outlying family field.
And in their turn the men gathered in carefully posted bands
with dogs
and shot the boars to death, every single one that moved
the small striped nimble piglets, the parturient sows
the black devils kill them, kill
ate their bodies and at St Senen used their hides
to fence a hen run against the foxes genets pole- and
    marten cats:
he had seen some remaining board-like tatters as he
    came:
he had remembered the strong dog a boar had disem-
    bowelled.
Crambs was his name, a dock-tailed hound that died,
    though carefully sewn up.

And the tales of men who had been served the same
    way out of life.

But it was in another age: at present he was lost.
Follow the coombe, you fool, he said, and walked along.
    Quite slowly now, an easy slope. Brown in ancient
    leaves: silent: a kind wood
with a silvery gentle light: bare soaring trunks, some
    very old indeed.
His disappointment faded as he walked along
No luck in girls at any time had he and his true expec-
    tation he never reached beyond good day
no factual good night at all
and in spite of a certain lowness and a pleasant languor
    filled him from head to foot.
Steadily on and on: no hurry now, and easy going, deep
    in wordless rumination on and on.
So quiet the wood that for perhaps an hour his own
    steps were all he heard until a rustling on his left
It was a marten crossing fallen leaves towards him: red
    coat, yellow white throat, brilliant chestnut eyes
    following its own road parallel to his: how he stared.
They crossed a few yards apart. It looked at him, with
    no particular emotion of any kind and they walked on.
He did not quite like to turn, feeling an absurd reversal
    of all principles
The marten cat, the wildest of all the wild wild creatures
    that ever starred
And this reversal was part of the day and this unknown
    silent wood

So that when a tall badger, reared against a tree-stump, a
    scratching-post, turned its striped head and glanced at
    him – but scratching still – he feigned an ignorance.
    Should he have called good day?
This was not the case when he came to the boars
Two boars. Two hundred pounds apiece, moving across
    towards some undergrowth
They turned on seeing him. Turned in a flash: enormous
    shoulders and dark heavy heads to gleaming tusks.
    Stood poised.
No question of good day. He sprang to a tree
    a tree of no great height alas but surely high enough:
    dropped his gun as he scrambled to the fork.
The boars stood still, while he sat panting in his fork.
And from the undergrowth, from between the trees,
    came other boars, some very large and darker still,
    some sows and smaller beasts: they came silently. And
    their square-cut flat snouts worked quick from side to
    side to catch his scent. He could hear their breath
He moved and they had gone, vanishing without a
    sound except for one young boar
    that crashed away.
A pause, and they were their again although he had not
    seen or heard them come
A ring right round the tree, and closing in: they all
    knew where he was.
Was his tree high enough? He had seen the marks of
    sharpened tusks a shocking height above the ground.
    And if high enough, would they ever go away?
No. They would not.

126

The two largest boars, followed by a close-packed band advanced deliberately.

'We don't mean no harm,' they said in a hoarse deep country voice

'You leave us alone, and we leave you alone. That's all we ask.'

'That's right,' said the powerful group behind.

'You just leave us alone, and we leave you alone,' said the leaders once again, in a surly, argumentative tone as though Martin had not agreed, had not already stated the gun was not his – a gun unloaded and for show

'That's all we have to say,' went on the boars. 'You treat us right:

we'll treat you right. That's all we have to say.'

'That's right,' said the rest, and they turned deliberately disappearing into the trees.

Night walkers

Walking on the

The long drought of summer

Drought all through the summer, no autumn rains
and the mountain burnt
the whole mountainside burnt. furrowed to the crest
It is dead and black now, so black
and like healing here I walk here in the darkness.
A long grind from the pass, going hard
and by the first milestone I am one step ahead of melancholy.
The level ground. the black road turning:
Sea on the left hand. far below, dim
and lighthouses flashing on the headlands.   Cap Béar, Canet, La Nouvelle
Just under the road small creatures rustle in the stones and the ashes
Shortly deliberately at intervals.
Three benighted partridges rocket from the scree above
pass overhead. clear against the sky.   There is a vixen belly for ahead: the milestone pass.
On to the one spring in this arid mountain
an improbable drip in the silence and here
shining block. blacker than the road. a Salamander
black with suspect golden blotches
we exchange looks by the light of a match
On and on. on and on. and at
last
it is the true rhythm: body facing steadily on
mind floating free. turning, musing, caressing a name
smiles to itself remembers
a thousand miles are dismissed. wiped out
and I sink deeper. hidden. warm
a dormouse in my secret love
      towards
      inward

inward warmth glow
dormouse
Salamander
lamasserai
lighthouse
Coral strand

Wilder shores

white stone

Paeonies

A long-deserted barracks
like a lamasery

conclusion
burrowing here e.d.

Night walking

Walking on the coral-strand
The long drought of summer
Drought all through the summer, no autumn rains
and the mountain burnt
the whole mountainside barren. Furious red to the crest
It is dead and black now, so black
and like healing like I walk there in the darkness
A long grind up from the pass, going hard
and by the first milestone I am one step ahead of
  melancholy.
The level ground, the black road turning:
Sea on the left hand, far below, dim
and lighthouses flashing on the headlands.
Just under this road 2 small creatures rustle in the
  stones and ashes
Snorting deliberately at intervals.
Three benighted partridges rocket from the scree above
pass overhead, clear against the sky.
There is a vixen calling far ahead: the white milestones
  pass.
On to the one spring in this arid mountain
all improbably drip in the silence and here
shining black, blacker than the road, a salamander
black with golden blotches
we exchange looks by the light of a match
On and on, on and on, and at
last
it is the true rhythm: feet beating steadily on
mind floating free, turning inwards musing, caressing a
  name

smiling to itself remembers
a thousand miles are dismissed, abolished
and I sink deeper, hidden, warm
a dormouse in my inward love

'On the mountain I have quite a good sense of direction'

On the mountain I have quite a good sense of direction
and on the dark bog too, going out for the dawn flighting.
But it does not answer in towns
and there where the grosvenors reared up their gallows
for the high justice rather than the low
which at the same time disappointed self-murdered
    lovers
were buried at the crossroads with a sharpened stake
ensuring that their hearts were really broken
there I say where the streets curve strangely
bend. change their names.

You can no more define love than you can define a feel of
youth

The True-born Englishman

(after Daniel Defoe)

The Romans first, with Julius Caesar came,
Including all the nations of that name.
Gauls, Greeks, and Lombards, and by computation
Auxiliaries or slaves, of every nation.
With Hengest, Saxons; Dames with Suens came;
In search of plunder, not in search of fame.
Scots, Picts, and Irish from the Hibernian shore;
And Conquering William brought the Normans o'er.

All these, their barbarous offspring left behind;
The dregs of armies, they, of all mankind:
Blended with Britons who before were here,
Of whom this Welsh have blessed the character.
From this amphibious ill-born mob began
That vain ill-natured thing, an Englishman.
Theft customs, surnames, languages, and manners
Of all these nations are their own explainers:
They have left a Shibboleth upon our tongue,
By which, with easy search, you may distinguish
Your Roman-Saxon-Danish-Norman/ English.

Thus from a mixture of all kinds began
That heterogeneous thing, an Englishman
In eager rapes and furious lust begot,
Betwixt a painted Britain and a Scot,
Whose gendering offspring quietly learned to bow
And yoke the heifers to the Roman plow.

A <u>True Born Englishman</u>'s a contradiction!
In speech an irony! In fact, a fiction!
A banter made to be a test of fools!
Which those that use it, justly ridicules.
A metaphor invented to express
A man akin to all the universe

Poverty has been much cried up
and as a school of holiness: no doubt it
And although

problems apparent

but when they are solved
The real problems appear

Sun sloping through the cypresses
bronze oranges ripen their tree.
Vineyards turning from green to gold
      on the turn
and away beyond the mountain with its far dark tower
The sea is also present. Half the landscape here is sea
calm today. with deep leaves wandering on the inverted sky:
a man could not scarcely ask a prettier confinement   exist
(unless he hankered wistlonger for a bog, snipe and wild swans   the smell of burning leaves
sighing on the soft rain, a trout-stream, the salmon running,
fox-hounds streaming off the line).   & a red fox running
But there is room enough between the oranges   something like
for the thin edge of despair comes through as smoothly as the sun.   despair to come   slip
In the best-appointed hermitage the man can ask
reflecting on his life may ask is this all?   his
And in spite of a feeling of abject ingratitude he may in time
repeat is this really all?
On the black day this might engulf him too   The answer could swallow
swallows him entirely with the answer yes certainly by all means if there were not   him entirely too
if it were not for a small private orchestra, a string quartet
playing away far down continually playing
                            street
about a bench overlooking a vast heavy odorous palace
walnuts. Gevrey-Chambertin. a warm kind dim warehouse
and the sound of morning crows.

134

'Sun sloping through the cypresses'

Sun sloping through the cypresses
bronze oranges upon their tree.
Vineyards on the turn from green to gold
and away beyond the mountain with its far dark tower
The sea is also present. Half the landscape here is sea
calm today, with deep laves wandering on the inverted sky:
a man could not ask a prettier confinement
(unless he [hankered] for a bog, snipe and wild swans
sighing in the soft rain, the smell of hickory leaves, a
    trout-stream the salmon running
fox-hounds striking off the line).
But there is room enough between the oranges
for the thin edge of something like despair to step
    through as smoothly as the sun
In the best appointed hermitage the man
reflecting on his life may ask, is this all?
And in spite of a feeling of abject ingratitude he may in time
repeat, is this really all?
On the black day this might engulf him too
swallow him entirely with the answer yes certainly
    by all means
if it were not for a small private orchestra, a string quartet
playing away far down continually playing
about a bench overlooking a vast great heavy ochreous
    palace
walnuts, Gevrey-Chambertin, a warm kind dun warehouse
and the sound of morning crows.

Labuntur anni (The advancing years)

The years flow by and
Presently you find
that with the sly gliding malevolence of dreams
those flowery meads
Lord lord those old flowery meads enamelled
have turned into a thin sheet of black ice thinner
in some places than others and everywhere unsafe
with here and there a pool open on to the void.
At intervals of staring you blunder on
the sheet growing thinner thinner mere webs of cold
and yourself dwindling in size virtue beauty sense
always on and on: no choice.

'Peace; a great lawn that small, fat feet'

Peace: a great lawn that small, fat feet
have trodden since the dawn of time
and still I tread it piping now
Space: Schubert floods the summer drawing room
spills into spreading the sunlit court.
Warmth. Driving slowly back from Mass and I see
the old claret-coloured roofs, the flowers
nestling below the forest and the sky
Roofs for old ways and kindness. hospitality.

The hard winter

The iron-faced plough-land, riven by the ice,
the unremitting wind too hard for snow.
Blue fieldfares scattered on the plough.
They lift and drift a foot and pitch
and watch you pass.
The red-wings died before them. They will die,
Both air and earth have joined with men
they cannot fight;
their god has fouled them, and the fieldfares cannot fly
the drifting flock of fieldfares from the north.

'An old thin tall man'

An old thin tall man
bent
his clothes are thick
his large and greyish stubbled face
bashed in by years
leads by the arch
leads in the sun
(he is the son)
a very old
and troubled man
there is no ugliness in piety
Anchises in his piety
to shudder is indecent then.

What the hell do you know about poverty?

Food, a warm bed and fire
A chair and a table
But food beyond everything
That is the basis
These are the great things.
Come, grow a sense of proportion.

'The north wind low over the house'

The north wind low over the house
And the sharp-winged peregrines passing low
The leaves fall, swirl aimlessly
Lie in unmoving heaps
The falcon clips through the wind to the South
autumn's lower turn
The lower edge of autumn

Where shall I find Spring?

'High on the cold mountain road'

High on the cold mountain road.
The path a little paler than the darkness
I hunt a poem through the night
Far far below the vast run of the curving sea
And on my right hand the tight-drawn mountains touch
remote Orion and the Pleiades.
But now I walk on thyme: thyme.
Thyme and the scent of grass
My thoughts drop from me like a shroud:
My heart is importuned by joy.

'I *went* out *in* a *night* of *tearing* wind'

I went out in a night of tearing wind
a warm gale from the south, tearing up the Spanish clouds.
There were no stars, no stars in the low sky
But then suddenly there was Venus, high and clear
    where the drift parted

So then we made a triangle
and its high sides were thirty million miles in length
its base a fortnight long.

                                    lifting to
                                    on the sun
A wheeling buzzard in the setting sun
gold in the light above the Llynau'r Cwm

The ravens barking on the sombre cliff
     you passed
the black wall of Cwm y Foel

A bitch fox screaming in the Ardda rocks
                                        wask
And on the still Llyn Adar ~~rings of rising trout~~
                            .
                          the evening rings of trout

    And on the secret Lake of Birds the evening rings of trout

A wheeling buzzard lifting to the sun
gold in the light above the Llynau'r Cwm.

The ravens barking on the sombre cliff
                          well
the ~~beneath black~~ of Cwm y Foel   (Black in the darkness of the Cwm y Fo

A bitch-fox screaming in the Ardda rocks
and on the naked ~~Lake of Bird~~ the rise and ring of trout
X The needless secret Lake of Birds is dappled with the rising fish
                                                              evening rise
X The rings are spreading on the sudden Lake of Birds
                                              silent
And rings are spreading crossing on the lake
and black the stirring water of the lake
Llyn Adar there. the black and silent lake.

                              144

'A wheeling buzzard lifting to the sun'

A wheeling buzzard lifting to the sun
gold in the light above the Llynau'r Cwm
The ravens barking on the sombre cliff
Black in the darkness of the Cwm y Foel
A bitch fox screaming in the Arddu rocks
Llyn Adar there, the black and silent lake.

'Thoughts that range from anger and revenge'

Thoughts that range from anger and revenge
to dread
And always this flayed heart and
straining ear
A hundred cars
But never ours. They turn.
Their engines die away.

'Of France and of the knowledge of that land'

Of France and of the knowledge of that land,
Of civil struggles and that Gallic band
That first in England strove, I sing.
May Chantecler inspire my lyre and bring
The numbers of my lab'ring verse and feet
To that smooth assonance that's sweet
For presentation verse: for know, O Bird.
That this attempt shall see no vulgar herd
But solely to the eye of M appear,
And for t'engage your better will I pray
You'll grace my pen: T'is for her festal day
And since no skilled artificer in gems or gold
Will in this merchants' town his stock unfold
Nor to his fellow cits but for ready money part.
Why then for birthday wares I to my heart
(a boundless purse for M) must start,
For my material wealth is shrunk so small
Nor may I, like Dan Chaucer, prince's bounty call
For present help, but either buy a bead
when she deserves an Orient pearl, or plead
The Gods' all-powerful aid, for O my masters
The poets that ye loved are gone and only poetasters
Are here to love and to be loved today.
Therefore, look kindly on your suppliant who kneels
For as your own true poets felt, he feels
And with your help he dreads not but he may
With pen his mistress please, not quite disgrace the day.

Captivity

Food, drink and women
there are chains.
Possessions, too.

Why add another? smoke?
smoke
food morning's gate
end and
the crown of meals
and evening's prize
chief adjutant of love and talk.
and hunger's step.

No doubt the hotel's very gay, though bound

and shrivelled tongue in dirtiness

Over all
the principle principall
Must smoke: an order, Diktat must.
be damned compulsion joy
besides
the shrivelled tongue, the dirty mouth
the dozen smoked in time
the craving out of time and place
to spoil the music, spoil the play the pictures

the running out
and shameful busy driven search for ends
that taste like hell.

This thing
that lend another barb to poverty
(as if it wanted more)
it is not fit.

The little red fox jumps over
Mary's ball pointed pen the same
thing
I am allowed to write with it
How kind

between my fingers as I
draw the little contracts
the glow is at my finger tips
I throw
the arc of shooting stars and dies
Farewell my sin, I have
enjoyed you

sibir

On my tripod exits a
woodbine!
Aricat serine and forni and
prophesy

wrecked tête-à-tête he
lacks a light

This is the last.
How sweet it draws
But gird your loins, my hero, high
upon this final tabbed prophecy
the coming joys of liberty

Captivity

Food, drink and women
these are chains.
Possessions, too
Why add another?
Smoke
Good morning's gate
the end and crown of meals
And swimming's prize
chief adjutant of love and talk
And hunger's stop.

Must smoke: an order, diktat, must
be damned compulsive joy
besides
the shrivelled tongue, the dirty mouth
the craving out of time and place
to spoil the music, spoil the play the pictures,
    manuscripts
wrecked tête à tête – he lacks a light
the running out
and shameful busy driven search for ends
that taste like hell.
This thing
that lends another barb to poverty
(as if it wanted more)
it is not fit.

This is the last
How sweet it draws
(was rolled with ease – foolish regretful fingers call)

But gird your loins, my hero: high
Upon this final tripod and prophesy
the coming joys of clear-eyed liberty.

'When a dry heart sets a bleeding'

When a dry heart sets a bleeding
then it pours, but an unmeaning liquor
more akin to gall.

Loud-mouthed neighbours through the floor

Bloody, bloody chattering.
Nothing to say and bursting with the saying of it
Spouting, bursting forth,
short-syllabled and chopped, elided, hard clacking, ~~hurried~~ hurried
Push forward, Importance
mouth apout, cheeks blowing: repetitious piffle
ten thousandth-hand opinion misconceived
burst in with it and interrupt
bear down and overlay that other voices
the whining one
The women never wholly stop
All rise and fall
- the least is loud -
and all unpleasant harsh and God damned apes.

Challenging and disagreeable
hard braying laughter sometimes
but
contentious, rising, and inimical

the BAHSTARDS.
they have nothing to say
they should exchange their meagre informations
(quietly)
and SHUT UP
Quiet quiet quiet, quiet
are you illiterate, can never think?
sit quiet and think?
Or go to sleep.

152

Loud-mouthed neighbours through the floor

Bloody, bloody chattering
Nothing to say and bursting with the saying of it
Spouting, bursting forth,
short-syllabled and chopped, elided, hard clacking,
    hurried
Challenging and disagreeable
hard braying laughter sometimes
but
contentious, rising and inimical
Push forward, importance
mouths apart, cheeks blowing, repetitious piffle
Ten thousandth-hand opinion misconceived
burst in with it and interrupt
bear down and overlay that other voice
the whining one
The women never wholly stop
All rise and fall
– the least is loud –
and all unpleasant harsh and God damned apes.

The BAHSTARDS.
They have nothing to say
they should exchange their meagre informations
(quietly)
and SHUT UP
Quiet quiet and quiet
are you illiterate, can never think?
sit quiet and think?
Or go to sleep.

'For Jojo's livre d'or 85'

A tight-packed village like a swarm of bees
The sea in three pure curves and they
divided by a holy lighthouse and
a vast great castle quite as old as time
A village loved by Matisse Picasso and the sun.
Down the middle runs a dried-up river-bed:
a street on its left hand, the aorta of the town:
on summer evenings the gentle flow
goes by perpetually, both to and fro
for this is where the village heart is found
a restaurant a café and a place
where you can eat like a lord or where
you and fishermen and masons may
play most passionately at cards
or sit
silently happy in the warmth
surrounded by the general sound of talk
while geckoes walk upon the wall
and the small owl calls gloc gloc.

Acknowledgements

HarperCollins *Publishers* gratefully acknowledges the assistance of Nikolai Tolstoy, Anastasia Elliot and Viktor Wynd in sourcing and transcribing many of the poems in this collection.

This is the last.
How sweet it draws
(was rolled with care — regretful foolish fingers care)
But gird your loins, my baboon: high
you this finest tripod
prophecy
the coming joys of clear-eyed liberty.

Between my fingers as I draw
the tide contracts
the glow is to my brown-stained thumb at last
I throw
the arc of shooting stars and lives
its gone. Farewell
farewell, my son
threw upon you.
farewell. good bye.

I will tell you something secretly in your ear. I die
but really like this tall gaunt thing loves. It looks
like the depression from a bubble made cotton paper. But
Roberta, stop Jane. Read one which came exactly like this.

Mary Bryand   NC MML MJ MCML
This, I believe, come from the imperfect enclosing of the
lines that comprise the ordinal letters.
I, for one, have to press hard, then I do it very very hard and open
Maria Bryand's Crème de Cacao e Maria Bryand's Crème de Cacao
Maria Bryand's Crème de Cacao e Maria Bryand's Crème de Cacao
Maria Bryand's Crème de Cacao Maria Bryand's Crème de Cacao
Maria Bryand's Crème de Cacao Maria Bryand's Crème de Cacao
It's a lonely form, God not. I hate it, I ask hoppers to k

Mighter Redwood
if you tall the sky
you will distinguish my
so soft awakened good

de Mary   Mary
It sighs à hille de Mary
Ballford, Mary

Farewell my son.   I have enjoyed you
Farewell my son.   I have enjoyed you
Farewell my son.   I have enjoyed you
Farewell my son.   I have enjoyed you
Farewell my son.

An old (tall) thin man
bent
with ugly clothes: his clothes are thick
his large and greyish stubble face
bashed in by years
lured by the arch
made in the sun
a very old
and doubled man
by turning shudder's out of place
the act is plain
filled with grace

they are not ugly

Index of first lines

All Attic virtues, beauty, wisdom, wit   6
Among the blacks the blue sea-captain stood   53
Beyond my window the mountain hangs like a curtain   18
blazing strand, A   33
Bloody, bloody chattering   153
boy – a man – I loved in County Down, A   44
burden of life too young, The   65
Charmed to be carrying the Cross that boy   83
Clouds over clouds, building up from
     in back of the mountain   95
Cold from the silent leaden sky, unmoving,
     full of snow   9
cry of buzzards in the sky, The   115
deep gold of a pomegranate-tree, The   22
dog bit his master, A   16
Down through the vines, the changing vines   99
femme qui chante, Une   15
flowering meads are very well: poets used often to
     commend, The   24
Food, a warm bed and fire   140
Food, drink and women   39, 149
Forbear O Venus pray forbear I read   117
Green bronze oranges round and hard on the thick
     branches   60
Hard running   45
harsh dry polished rattle of the palm fronds, The   7
He had dispossessed them of their land   78
Help my understanding, Lady   98
High on the cold mountain road   142

Hurrying through the streams of grey,
    upslanting people   40
I am poor about loving, so   12
I had never supposed green eyes had charms   38
I too walked in churchyards and spelt out the stones   20
I was young and read a poem   76
I went out in a night of tearing wind   143
I went up to the Consolation   55
If I could go back into my dream   102
In the dark of the night before the moon rose they went
    down the worn road   67
In the Place, naked lights hang in the trees   109
Inventing, she added a pinch to the mixture   81
iron-faced plough-land, riven by the ice, The   138
Is true the rat   86
Long ago I planted cypress seeds   23
Long, straight, the steel lines   101
Loose-bellied, grey, cross, absolute   103
Mad women, talking inwards, crazed, and   70
man long used to affection (a roof, as it were, A   17
Mists after mountain rain   37
My youth   47
No, they said at the post, there is nothing. There is
    nothing for that name   58
north wind low over the house, The   141
Not that a hard-roed herring should presume   113
O see the shiners   72
octopus: there is the beast of all creatures, The   88
Of France and of the knowledge of that land   147
old thin tall man, An   139
On the edge of the sea, no stir   62
On the far side of the pass it was still night   32
On the left hand the sea   85

On the mountain I have quite a good sense
    of direction   131
pattering of rain, The   114
Peace: a great lawn that small, fat feet   137
people of this [Chelsea ambulance] station
    are disconsolate and rude, The   1
Pilgrims coming from the west side   36
present is chiefly a fragment, a token, A   13
raven of the Pyrenees, The   64
red haired head with close-set shallow eyes, A   71
Romans first, with Julius Caesar came, The   132
sea and the sky are silent, The   5
She asked me did I love her   73
She had not pulled a root, a root   92
Sink. down in the grey sea   43
snow has almost vanished from Las Nao Fons, The   21
Sun sloping through the cypresses   135
Tartar cleared the table, drank up the madeira sauce, A   118
Test, broad on this lower stretch and placid, The   34
There was a lane behind the gasworks, they said   27
Think of me   91
This city afternoon   89
Thoughts that range from anger and revenge   146
Three men sitting in a room on the second floor   28
tight-packed village like a swarm of bees, A   154
To bed with slow acid dripping toward one's head   120
town takes on its antique darkness, The   46
Trees rising straight without the least transition   94
unexpected patch of brown, the ploughland, The   41
Up and up, perpetually climbing, up   121
Upon a shallow bay the sun, the sacred phallus   100
vent qui chant dans le bois des oiseaux   14
Vicious intromission is a legal term   116

vignes, les chênes-lièges, oliviers et thym, Les   14
vines, the cork trees, olives and the thyme, The   82
Virtue's self, I have not yet   48
Waking to the knowledge that I must not smoke   90
Walking on the coral-strand   129
Walking on the high mountain – the path   97
We are old bald ugly   104
We have a shifting population of flamingoes   25
We looked over the cliff and there were foxes   19
wheeling buzzard lifting to the sun, A   145
When a dry heart sets a bleeding   151
When my Muse and Chian Veins vie   119
When your lance fails   105
Whereas in Jewry came a star   112
'wine-dark sea' a commonplace?, The   69
winter hillside, The   11
With ash on your love   75
woman singing, A   52
wood of birds, The   66
years flow by and, The   136
Yesterday an old husband   111
You clear the shallow earth away   30
You lie there unmoving   87
You will come to it   8
Your workman, the one with the pulley on Thursday   49